P9-DFV-055

PUBLIC LIBRARY
Stoneham, Mass.

Cat Up a Tree

John and Ann Hassett

HOUGHTON MIFFLIN COMPANY BOSTON

Walter Lorraine Books

Walter Lorraine (wл) Books

Copyright © 1998 by John and Ann Hassett
All rights reserved. For information about permission
to reproduce selections from this book, write to
Permissions, Houghton Mifflin Company, 215 Park
Avenue South, New York, New York 10003.
Library of Congress Cataloging-in-Publication Data
Hassett, John.
 Cat up a tree / written and illustrated by John and Ann Hassett.
  p. cm.
 Summary: With rapidly increasing numbers of cats stuck in her
tree, Nana Quimby asks for help from the firehouse, the police, the
pet shop, the zoo, the library, and even city hall, but no one will
help rescue the cats.
 ISBN 0-395-88415-2
 [1. Cats — Fiction. 2. City and town life — Fiction.] I. Hassett,
Ann (Ann M.) II. Title.
PZ7.H2785Cat 1998
[E] — dc21   97-47276
                        CIP
                        AC

Printed in the United States of America
HOR 10 9 8 7 6 5 4 3 2

Cat Up a Tree

Nana Quimby went to the window
and saw a cat up a tree.
She rang the firehouse on her telephone.
"Help!" she cried. "Cat up a tree."

"Sorry," said the firehouse, "we do not catch cats up a tree anymore. Call back if that cat starts playing with matches."

Nana Quimby went to the window and counted five cats up the tree.
She rang the police station. "Help!" she cried. "Five cats up a tree."

"Sorry," said the police station, "we do not catch cats up a tree.
Call back if the cats rob a bank."

Nana Quimby went to the window and counted ten cats up the tree.
She rang the pet shop. "Help!" she cried. "Ten cats up a tree."

"Sorry," said the pet shop, "we do not catch cats up a tree.
Call back if the cats wish to buy a dog."

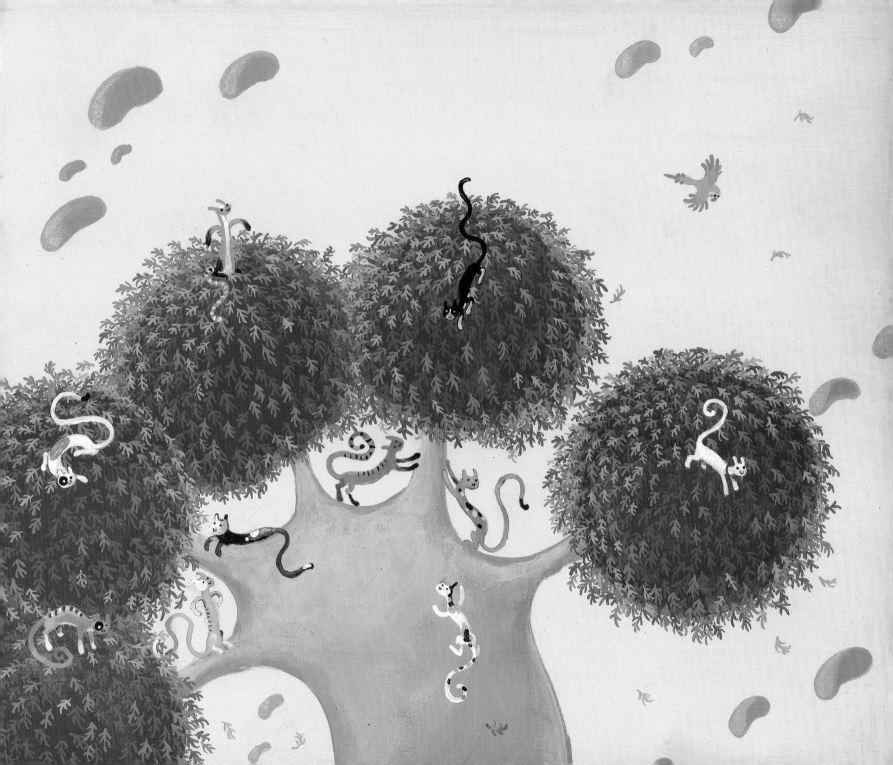

Nana Quimby went to the window and counted fifteen cats up the tree. She rang the zoo. "Help!" she cried. "Fifteen cats up a tree."

"Sorry," said the zoo, "we do not catch cats up a tree. Call back if one of the cats is tall and has stripes — our tiger is missing."

Nana Quimby went to the window and counted twenty cats up the tree. She rang the post office. "Help!" she cried. "Twenty cats up a tree."

"Sorry," said the post office, "we do not catch cats up a tree. Call back if the cats are sending a postcard and need a stamp."

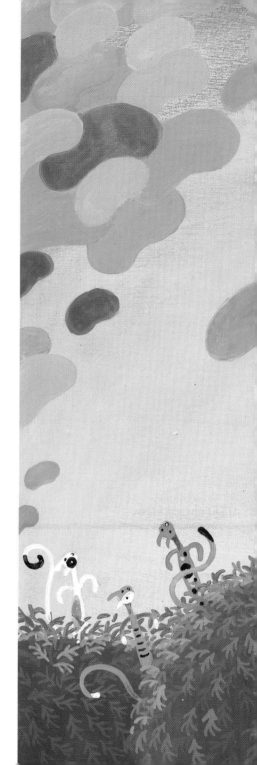

Nana Quimby went to the window and counted twenty-five cats up the tree. She rang the library. "Help!" she cried. "Twenty-five cats up a tree."

"Sorry," said the library, "we do not catch cats up a tree. Call back if the cats have an overdue book."

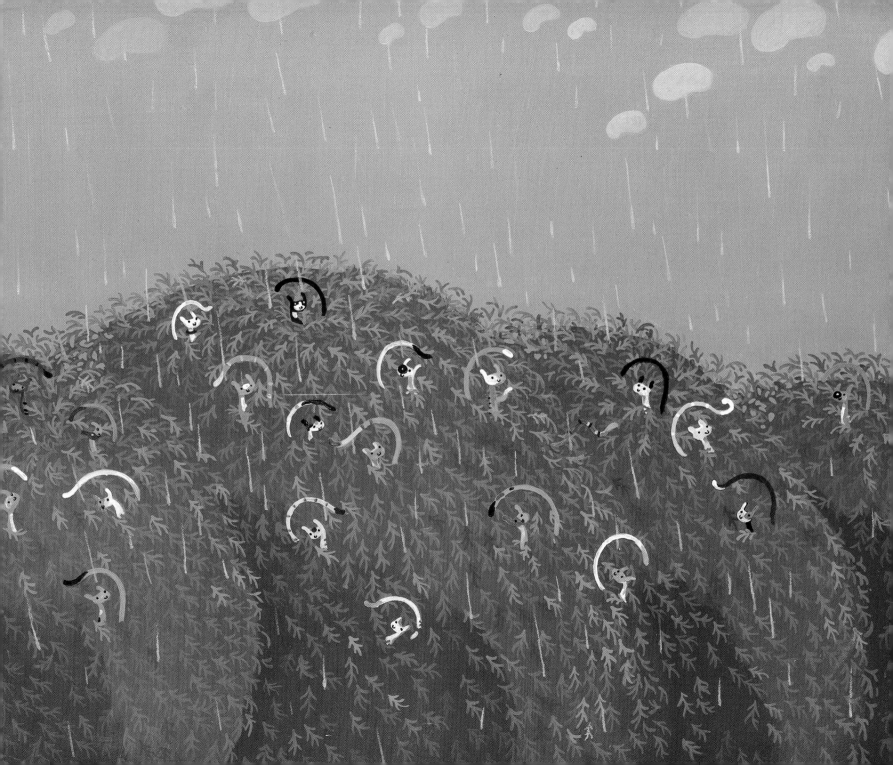

Nana Quimby went to the window and counted thirty cats up the tree.

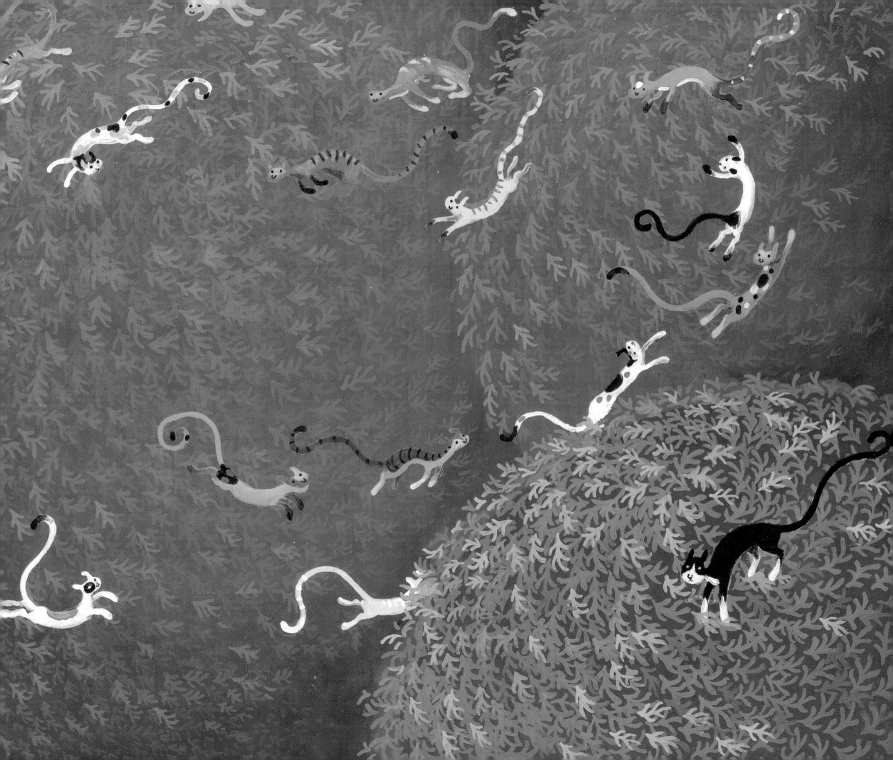

She rang city hall. "Help!" she cried. "Thirty cats up a tree."

"Sorry," said city hall, "we do not catch cats up a tree. Call back if you need a sign that says Danger! Look up for Falling Cats."

So when Nana Quimby went to the window and counted thirty-five cats

up the tree, she threw the telephone out the window.

Then forty cats tiptoed across the telephone line and hopped in the window into Nana Quimby's arms.

Later, Nana Quimby's telephone rang — it was city hall!

"*Help!*" cried city hall.
"*Mice in the firehouse,*
mice in the jail,
mice in books,
mice in the mail.
Mouse here,
mouse there —
millions of mouses
EVERYWHERE!"

"Sorry," said Nana Quimby, "the cats do not catch mice anymore.
Call back if you wish to hear cats *purr.*"
She set the phone down softly, for too many cats to count
were having a nap.

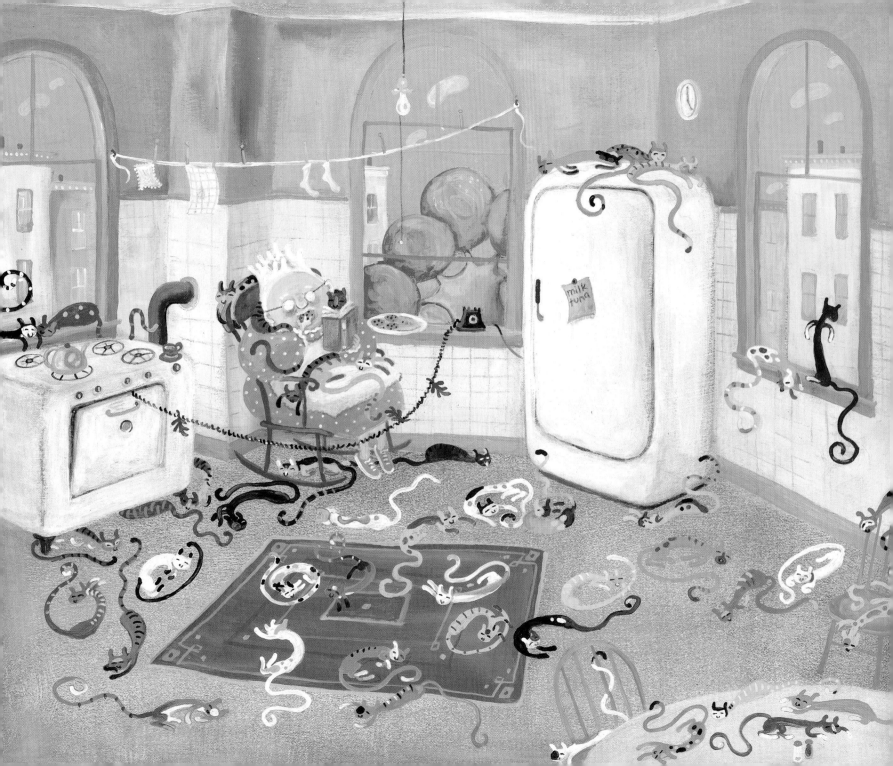

For Michael, David, Ryan, Torrie, Jackie, Bobby, and Lauren

JE
Community Helpers Kit

STONEHAM PUBLIC LIBRARY

3 1509 00545 5459

JUNIOR ROOM
PUBLIC LIBRARY
Stoneham, Mass.